KARA MAY

Big Puss,
Little Mouse

Illustrated by Susie Jenkin-Pearce

Hippo

For Jo and Dido's Albert.

Scholastic Children's Books,
Commonwealth House, 1-19 New Oxford Street,
London WC1A 1NU, UK
a division of Scholastic Ltd
London ~ New York ~ Toronto ~ Sydney ~ Auckland

Published in the UK by Scholastic Ltd, 1997

Text copyright © Kara May, 1997
Illustrations copyright © Susie Jenkin-Pearce, 1997

ISBN 0 590 13641 0

Typeset by Backup... Creative Services, Dorset
Printed by Cox & Wyman Ltd, Reading, Berks.

10 9 8 7 6 5 4 3 2 1

Big Puss, Little Mouse

"Hey, Big Puss, it's me! Here I am! Look!"

Big Puss froze where he stood. He was a very big cat but he was very scared of mice! At the sight of Little Mouse jumping about right under his nose:

his fur stood on end

his tummy whizzed round

his heart went **thump! thump! thump!**

Another *wonderful* Young Hippo Animal story for animal-lovers!

Hands Off Our Hens!
Jennifer Curry

Join the Petsitters Club for *more* animal adventure!

1. Jilly the Kid
2. The Cat Burglar
3. Donkey Rescue
Tessa Krailing

These Young Hippo Magic stories are fantastic!

My Friend's a Gris-Quok
Malorie Blackman

Diggory and the Boa Conductor
The Little Pet Dragon
Philippa Gregory

Broomstick Services
Ann Jungman

The Cleaning Witch
Cecilia Lenagh

Hello Nellie and the Dragon
Elizabeth Lindsay

The Marmalade Pony
Linda Newbery

Mr Wellington Boots
Ann Ruffell

The Wishing Horse
Malcolm Yorke

Chapter 1

Big Puss, Scaredy Cat

Big Puss lived with Mrs Petal. He'd lived with her since he was a kitten.

"I'm not a kitten now, Mrs Petal," Big Puss said one morning.

Mrs Petal gave a smile. She knew what Big Puss meant. He meant that he wanted a big breakfast! She gave him a tin of cat food, some biscuits and a bowl of milk. Soon he'd licked the plates clean.

"You're even bigger now," said Mrs Petal.

Big Puss looked at his tum. It was so full with breakfast he was afraid it might burst.

"I don't want a burst tum! I'd better walk some breakfast off," he said. "See you later, Mrs Petal."

He got up with a stretch and walked into the garden. It was a large garden and he loved it. He headed straight for the roses and took a sniff at every one. Then he strolled around the apple tree. He peered up through the branches.

Those apples are ripe for picking. I must remember to tell Mrs Petal, Big Puss thought.

He went on his way past the flower-beds to where the garden grew wild. Mrs Petal called it "A Mess". Big Puss called it "The Jungle". It was the part of the garden he loved best. Every time he went there, he felt he was setting off on an adventure. His thoughts were far away, wondering what today's adventure would be, when he felt something tickle his tail. He knew who it was. It was Little Mouse. She scampered round and waved her arms in front of him.

"Hey, Big Puss, it's me! Here I am! Look!"

Big Puss froze where he stood. He was a very big cat but he was very scared of mice! At the sight of Little Mouse jumping about right under his nose:

his fur stood on end

his tummy whizzed round

his heart went **thump! thump! thump!**

Little Mouse knew how scared Big Puss was of mice. Her mouse-mates kept their distance. After all, he was a very big cat! But she was mischievous and daring and liked to show off to the others that she could scare him all the more, even though she was only a little mouse.

"Hey, you lot, watch this!"

She jumped on to Big Puss's tail and ran up and down it as if it were a motorway.

"Brrrm! Brrrm!" went Little Mouse.

Big Puss just stood where he was. He longed to run, but fear kept him rooted to the spot.

"Please go away," he trembled.

Little Mouse giggled, her face bright with mischief.

"Hey, Big Puss, do you know what I'm going to do next?"

Big Puss hoped she'd say she was going to go home, now, at once! But Little Mouse moved in closer.

"I'm going to jump on your head and tickle your ears, that's what!"

She was about to jump when her mates gave a warning cry. Little Mouse

looked round to see Sam and
Veronica, the Siamese twins, leap
down from next door's fence. Unlike
Big Puss, they weren't scared of mice.

"Hey you lot, let's go!" shouted
Little Mouse.

The mice raced off. Sam and Veronica bounded after them. "Let's go get 'em!" they screeched. Big Puss watched after them. He longed to go-get the mice with Sam and Veronica.

"That's what cats do and I should do it too. I wish I wasn't me," he sighed. "I wish I wasn't scared of mice, but I am! Oh, dear! Oh, dear!" A tear rolled down his face. Sadly, he turned to go indoors. But just then, Sam and Veronica came running back. Little Mouse and the others had given them the slip.

"But we'll get 'em one day," said Sam.

"At least we *tried* to get 'em, which is more than you did, Big Puss," said

Veronica. "Two of us make one of you but we're not scared of mice."

"There's no need to go on and on," said Big Puss.

But Sam and Veronica enjoyed making fun of him.

"A mouse can't eat you," said Sam. "Next to you, Big Puss, a mouse is a flea and you're an elephant!"

"You're the only cat in the street, in the town, in the WORLD who's scared of mice," put in Veronica.

"There are lots of things I'm *not* scared of," said Big Puss, trying to cheer himself up. "I'm not scared of Mrs Petal's growly-growly grass cutter. I'm not scared of roaring thunder. I'm not even scared of Sharp-tooth Fox. I always chase him off."

"Never mind what you're NOT scared of. You're scared of mice!" jeered Sam and Veronica.

They danced round and chanted:

"*Big Puss is a big cat*
He's scared of little mice.
Big Puss is a scaredy cat
Mice give him a fright."

They chanted it over and over again. Big Puss just stood there, too upset to go for them. Besides, he thought, what they were saying was true and he couldn't deny it. The best he could do was to be brave when they jeered at him and try not to cry. At last, however, Mrs Petal came out to hang up the washing.

"That will do," she said sternly to Sam and Veronica. Sam and Veronica fell silent at once but Big Puss felt even more ashamed.

"I shouldn't need you to stick up for me, Mrs Petal. I'm a big cat, a very big cat, and I shouldn't be scared of mice."

Mrs Petal tried to comfort him. "Never mind, Big Puss. You can't help it," she said.

"But I *do* mind," said Big Puss. "What's more," he went on, "I've got to do something about it and I will."

"About time!" sniffed Sam.

"What are you going to do?" sneered Veronica.

Big Puss stopped to think. "Instead of me being scared of mice," he said at last, "I'll make them scared of me!"

"When?" asked Sam.

"In a million years' time?" scoffed Veronica.

"No. Today! I'm going to find a mouse and scare it right now."

Big Puss drew himself up to his biggest and strode off with his head held high, leaving Mrs Petal and Sam and Veronica watching after him.

"The next mouse I see had better watch out!" he said.

He went striding on down through The Jungle till he came to a grassy bank at the end of Mrs Petal's garden. It sloped steeply down to a stream below. Big Puss gave a shiver. He hated getting wet and just to look at all that water made his skin feel clammy.

"Ooh-er! Ooh-er!" he said.

But he hadn't come here to shiver by the water. He'd come to look for a mouse to scare and he knew just where he'd find one. On the other side of the stream was a field. He called it the Mouse Field because Little Mouse and her mates and lots of other mice lived there. He'd never been there, not once, but now he went striding on towards the wooden bridge that went across the stream.

"I told Sam and Veronica I'd find a mouse and scare it and that's what I'm going to do!" said Big Puss, and he went boldly on across the bridge towards the Mouse Field.

Chapter 2

Big Puss in the Mouse Field

Big Puss took another step along the bridge and there he was, in the Mouse Field. The ground under his feet didn't feel full of danger. It felt quite ordinary, just like the ground in Mrs Petal's garden. But this wasn't Mrs Petal's garden. This was the Mouse Field!

"The Mouse Field!" trembled Big

Puss. "Ooh-err! Oooh-errr! Ooooh-errrr!"

Saying he was going to give the first mouse he saw "what for" was one thing, doing it was something else! Now he was in the Mouse Field, at just the thought of a mouse, all pointed nose and string-like tail:

his fur stood on end
his tummy whizzed round
his heart went **thump! thump! thump!**

Big Puss was dismayed. "Oh, dear! Oh, dear!" he said. "I've not even seen a mouse yet and look at the state I'm in. I can't unscare myself of mice however hard I try. Sam and Veronica will make fun of me for ever." He gave a sigh, a long, sad sigh. But suddenly it turned into a grin. Big Puss had an idea.

"If I don't *see* a mouse," he said, "then I can't scare it. Not even Sam and Veronica will say that I can."

Not seeing a mouse was easy.

"I'll shut my eyes," said Big Puss.

He shut his eyes tightly. If a mouse was about he wouldn't see it.

But I might hear it, he thought. I'd better sing my loudest, I won't hear it then. And so I won't smell it, I'll screw up my nose.

His singing sounded like a foghorn, coming through his screwed-up nose, but he wasn't bothered.

"I'd rather hear me making a din than hear a mouse squeak!"

Big Puss stood there for a moment with his eyes shut, his nose screwed up and singing, "Tra la la la la." He felt a bit of a nerd but at least he'd be able to tell Sam and Veronica he hadn't scared a mouse today because he hadn't seen or heard or smelled one to scare.

And what's more, he thought, it'll be the truth and not a lie.

He decided to stay in the Mouse Field for a while, then he'd go home. But it was boring to stand in one place. It would make the time go more quickly if he walked around. He took one careful step, then another. Soon he got used to walking without seeing where he was going, so he went faster, head first into a blackberry bush!

"Ouch!" he yelped. "I'm being prickled!"

It took ages to unprickle himself with his eyes shut, but he didn't dare to open his eyes in case he saw a mouse. At last he managed to free himself and walk on. He'd gone just a few steps when he felt his feet sink into something squishy. SQUISH! It was an extra-large cow-pat. Big Puss paused.

"Mmm!" he said. "Mmm!" he said again. "There's something squishy underfoot!"

He was tempted to look, or at least take a sniff to see what he was standing in. But he decided to stick to his plan and keep his eyes shut, his nose screwed up, and sing his loudest till he was safely out of the Mouse Field.

He'd just pulled his feet out of the cow-pat when Little Mouse and her mates came running. They'd heard the singing and were astonished to see it was Big Puss.

"What's he doing here, in our field?" wondered Little Mouse.

"Perhaps he's come to gobble you up to pay you back for teasing him!" said the others.

Little Mouse laughed. "Big Puss? He'd never dare." She ran up and made a face at him.

"Hey there, Big Puss."

Big Puss walked calmly on. She realized his eyes were shut and he hadn't seen her. "There's a puzzle here," she said. "Why would he walk about with his eyes shut?"

"And he's got his nose screwed up," said the others. "And he's singing too!"

Little Mouse nodded. "If you can call that horrible noise singing," she said. "Let's follow him for a bit and see what he does."

Big Puss walked on and Little Mouse and the others walked behind him.

He didn't realize he'd turned back on himself and was now near the steep bank of the stream. Just ahead was a tree. It was the only tree that grew in the field. Little Mouse giggled.

"Hey, you lot, I'm going to have some fun!"

"What sort of fun?" asked the others.

Little Mouse ran on and up the tree. "When Big Puss walks underneath, I'll jump on his head and shout, 'Boo!' He'll open his eyes and see me. Then:

his fur will stand on end

his tummy will go whizzing

his heart will **thump!**

"Here he comes! Watch!"

Little Mouse peered down, ready to jump, as Big Puss walked on towards the tree. It was a day of hot sun. He was surprised when he felt a sudden chill. He didn't realize it was a branch blocking out the sun. Perhaps it was going to rain, he thought. Rain would be a good excuse to go home. Even Sam and Veronica ran indoors at the first raindrop and they wouldn't expect him to stay out in a cloudburst. He decided to take a quick peek to see if there were any clouds about. Mice didn't live in the sky so there wasn't any risk of seeing one.

Big Puss opened his eyes and looked up.

At just that moment Little Mouse jumped.

"Hey, it's me, Big Puss!"

Big Puss's scream burst across the Mouse Field.

"Ahhhhh!"

Can YOU read four Young Hippo books?

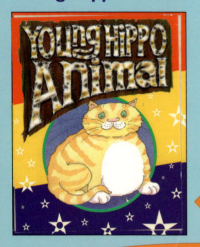

The Young Hippo is sending a special prize to everyone who collects any four of these stickers, which can be found in Young Hippo books.

This is one sticker to stick on your own Young Hippo Readometer Card!

Collect four stickers and fill up your Readometer Card

There are all these stickers to collect too!

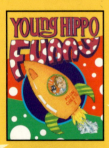

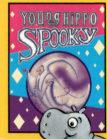

Get your Young Hippo Readometer Card from your local bookshop, or by sending your name and address to:

Young Hippo Readometer Card Requests, Scholastic Children's Books, 6th Floor, Commonwealth House, 1-19 New Oxford Street, London WC1A 1NU

Offer begins March 1997

This offer is subject to availability and is valid in the UK and the Republic of Ireland only.

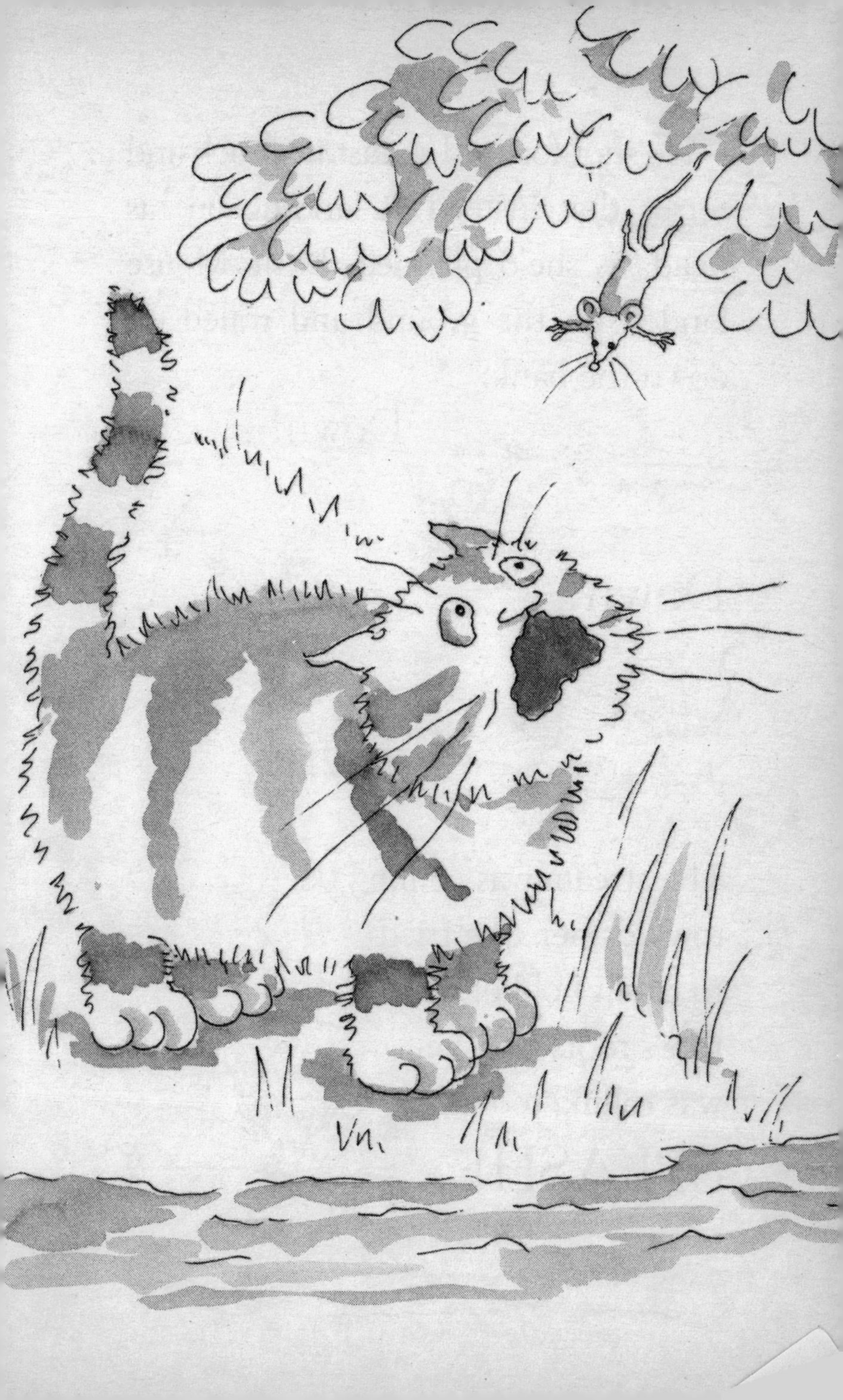

He shot forward so fast in shock and terror that instead of landing on his head, as she'd planned, Little Mouse landed on the ground and rolled on down the bank.

Down!

Down!

Down!

The stream was coming towards her. She tried to catch hold of the tree's roots but she was rolling too fast.

SPLASH!

Little Mouse felt the water close over her. She struggled to the surface.

"Help!" she spluttered. "I can't swim!"

The other mice scrambled down to the edge of the stream. They couldn't swim either. They stretched out their arms to try to pull her out.

"We can't reach you, Little Mouse. We'll have to get help. Kick your feet and splash your arms and try to stay afloat!"

They ran back up to the top of the bank and looked round in a panic. There was no one in sight. Then they caught sight of Big Puss. In his fear he'd bolted head first into a rabbit hole.

"Come on!" squeaked the mice.
"Let's get him!"

Big Puss heard the patter of their little mousy feet. He tried to back away, further down the rabbit hole.

"Oh, no!" he groaned. "I'm stuck."

"We'll unstick you," said the mice.
"Altogether now!"

They took hold of his tail and pulled.

Big Puss shot out like a cork from a bottle. The mice managed to jump aside just in time or he'd have landed SQUASH! on top of them. Before he could make his escape, the mice gathered round. Big Puss was surrounded by pointed mousy noses and twitchy mousy whiskers.

"Oooh-err! Please go away!" he trembled.

But the mice moved in towards him.

"Little Mouse is drowning! It's life or death! Please save her, Big Puss!"

"Life or death!" exclaimed Big Puss. He was a big cat, a very big cat. Just this once, he told himself:

"I WON'T BE SCARED OF MICE."

He raced on down the bank. There

was Little Mouse, swirling in the water. Big Puss stopped and stared. His burst of courage left him. At the sight of Little Mouse his fear of mice came rushing back:

his fur stood on end
his tummy whizzed round
his heart went **thump! thump! thump!**

Little Mouse gave a desperate, spluttery cry.

"Help! Save me!"

Big Puss knew what he should do, but could he do it? He was as scared of mice as ever.

Chapter 3

Big Puss, Little Mouse

Big Puss stood, staring down into the stream. All he saw now of Little Mouse was a small scared face with huge scared eyes. It was the scared eyes that did it!

"I can't let her drown!" Big Puss said.

He bounded down to the edge of the stream. He could stretch further than the mice but not far enough to reach Little Mouse.

"Hold me, mice," he said. "Then I'll be able to reach further."

They held his back legs and his tail.

"We've got you, Big Puss! Have another go!"

Big Puss tried again. Little Mouse was still out of reach. If he was to save her, he'd have to go into the stream. But he'd never learnt to swim and how he hated getting wet!

"This isn't the time to fuss about that, Big Puss," he told himself. "This is a time of life or death!"

He stepped into the water.

"I'm coming, Little Mouse!"

The stream was drowning-deep for Little Mouse. He wondered if it'd be drowning-deep for him too! But he wouldn't think about that! He was a big cat, a very big cat. Now he must be a brave cat too!

He waded on through the stream.

SPLISH! SPLASH! The water soaked through his fur and made it heavy. It was like wearing a soggy suit of armour and it slowed him down. With every step, the stream was getting deeper. Big Puss paused.

If I go any further, he thought, it might come over my head!

But Little Mouse was sinking. He could only see her ears. He took another step. The water rushed over him. It was in his eyes, in his mouth, in his nose.

"This is no time to panic!" Big Puss told himself firmly.

He stood up on tiptoe. He was coughing up water but his head was in the clear. He reached out with his very longest stretch. A cheer went up from the bank.

"He's got Little Mouse!"

Big Puss felt her tremble.

"It's all right, Little Mouse, I'm not going to hurt you," he said.

Carefully, very carefully, he carried her ashore. The others gathered round, all a-squeak with shock as he put her gently on the grass.

"There you are, Little Mouse, safe on dry land."

Little Mouse shivered. "I was scared I'd drown. Now I'm so c-cold I'm s-scared I'll freeze to death."

"I'll soon warm you up," said Big Puss.

He licked her dry in no time at all.

Little Mouse began to cry. Tears trickled down her nose. "What's up, Little Mouse?" he asked. "You're not cold or drowning now. There's no need to cry."

"Yes, there is," sniffled Little Mouse. "I'm crying from shame. Shame that I was mean and teased you," she said. "If you'd let me drown or freeze to death it would have been my fault."

"Yes, it would!" the others chimed in.

"If you were Sam and Veronica, you'd eat me," went on Little Mouse. "But you won't, will you?" she pleaded.

Big Puss gave a grin. "There's not enough of you to eat, you're such a little mouse! To think I was so scared of you that my fur stood up, my tummy whizzed round and my heart went thump! It makes me want to laugh.

"Ha! ha! ha!" laughed Big Puss.

Little Mouse began to laugh too and so did the others. But suddenly their laughter stopped as they caught sight of Sam and Veronica. They'd slunk up, unnoticed, through the tall grass. Now they circled round the mice with a stare that held them frozen. Even Little Mouse froze with terror where she stood.

"Watch this, Scaredy Cat!" said Sam.

"We'll show you how to scare mice!" said Veronica.

They moved in towards the mice.

Their blue eyes glinted. They arched their backs to pounce.

"Hold it right there," rapped out Big Puss. "Take one more step and you've had it!" He drew himself up and hissed. Sam and Veronica paused. It was two against one. But Big Puss was a very big cat and now he looked very fierce.

"Whatever's going on!"

It was Mrs Petal. She'd seen Big Puss then the other two cats heading for the Mouse Field, and was worried there might be trouble.

"Well, what's going on?" she asked again.

Big Puss shuffled his feet. Sam and Veronica looked at the ground.

"I'll tell you, Mrs Petal!" piped up
Little Mouse. "First, I nearly got
drowned but Big Puss saved me. Then
Sam and Veronica were going to get
us but Big Puss wouldn't let them
because he's my friend, aren't you, Big
Puss?"

Big Puss didn't pause. "Yes, I am," he
said.

Sam and Veronica gasped in astonishment. "But you're scared of mice, Big Puss."

"No, he's not!" retorted Little Mouse.

To prove her point, she jumped on his back. "Hi there, Big Puss," she said.

"Hi there, Little Mouse," grinned Big Puss.

The other mice jumped up too.

"I'll take you for a ride, if you want," said Big Puss.

Little Mouse and the others held on tight. "Off you go, Big Puss."

He raced up and down, through the tall grass. Mrs Petal waved but Sam and Veronica huffed in annoyance.

First Big Puss was scared of mice, which no cat should be. Now he was friends with mice, which cats shouldn't be either.

"But he's having all the fun!" said Sam.

"It's not fair!" said Veronica.

Sam and Veronica slunk off. Then, soon after, the mice had to go home too. Their mums and dads were calling.

"Hadn't you better go too, Little Mouse?" asked Mrs Petal. "Won't your mum and dad be worried?"

Little Mouse shook her head. "I haven't got a mum and dad, I've only got me. I live by myself."

"By yourself!" said Big Puss. He couldn't believe it. "But you're such a little mouse!" He looked at Mrs Petal. Mrs Petal nodded.

"You can come and live with us! If you want to, that is," said Big Puss.

"I do! Oh, yes, I do!" Little Mouse jumped about with joy. "You're the very best cat-friend a mouse could ever have!" She ran up his tail and sat on his head.

"Hey, Big Puss, do you know what?"

"What?" asked Big Puss.

She bent down and whispered in his ear.

"I'm glad I'm not scaring you any more, that's what!"

"So am I!" grinned Big Puss.

"Come along, you two, let's have lunch," said Mrs Petal.

The three of them had lunch together, in the shade of a tree, outdoors on the patio. Mrs Petal gave a smile.

"I always wanted a cat who was friends with mice," she said. "I never thought that cat would be you, Big Puss."

"Nor did I!" said Big Puss. "And there's something else I thought I'd never do. But I'm going to do it. I'll tell you what it is!"

He told Little Mouse and Mrs Petal.

"That's a genius idea. We'll do it today," said Little Mouse.

Later that afternoon Big Puss and Little Mouse set off towards the stream. Sam and Veronica came snooping by. They couldn't believe what they saw! Little Mouse and Big Puss were splashing about in the water.

"We're learning to swim. My friend

Big Puss said we should so we won't get drowned. So there!" said Little Mouse.

"Come and join us!" Big Puss said.

Sam and Veronica took one look at the water, turned tail and raced off.

"They're scaredy cats," said Little Mouse. "Scared of a bit of water! Not like us, Big Puss. But now my tummy's hungry. Do you think it could be teatime?"

Big Puss laughed. "You sound just like me! Come on, let's go and see."

Little Mouse jumped on his back and they went on home to Mrs Petal, feeling pleased with themselves and with each other.

The End